BRIGHT and EARLY Books
for BEGINNING Beginners

This book belongs to...

_____

© Illus. Dr. Seuss 1957

Originally published in a different form by Random House, Inc., New York, and in
Canada by Random House of Canada Limited, Toronto ISBN 0-679-89462-4 (trade) —
ISBN 0-679-99462-9 (lib. bdg.).

BRIGHT & EARLY BOOKS and colophon and RANDOM HOUSE and colophon are registered
trademarks of Random House, Inc.

SCHOLASTIC and associated logos are trademarks and/or registered trademarks of
Scholastic Inc.

This BOOK CLUB EDITION published by Scholastic Inc.
90 Old Sherman Turnpike, Danbury, Connecticut 06816.

ISBN 0-7172-6781-4

Printed in the U.S.A.

First Scholastic printing, March 2003

Mama
Loves

By Molly Goode
Illustrated by Lisa McCue

A Bright & Early Book
From Beginner Books
A Division of Random House, Inc.

SCHOLASTIC Book Club Edition

Mama loves.

Mama loves you,
little one.

Mama loves
her baby so,
as you play
in the water.

But if ever
there is danger,
she will hug
her little daughter.

Mama loves.

Mama takes you
to the river
and teaches you
when you are young.

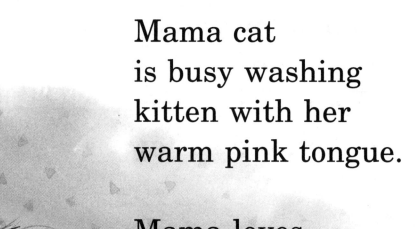

Mama cat
is busy washing
kitten with her
warm pink tongue.

Mama loves.

Mama loves you,
little calf,
and takes you up
to breathe the air.

Baby panda's
never sad,
for mama panda's
always there.

Mama loves you,
little one.
It's time to show you
how to swim.

But if baby
does not want to . . .

. . . Mama will
just push you in!

Mama loves.

Mama's ducklings,
one day old,
have webby feet
and down so fine.

Mama goes
to take a walk,
and you all follow
in a line.

Mama's own
dear little one,
you drink your milk
and stand so tall!

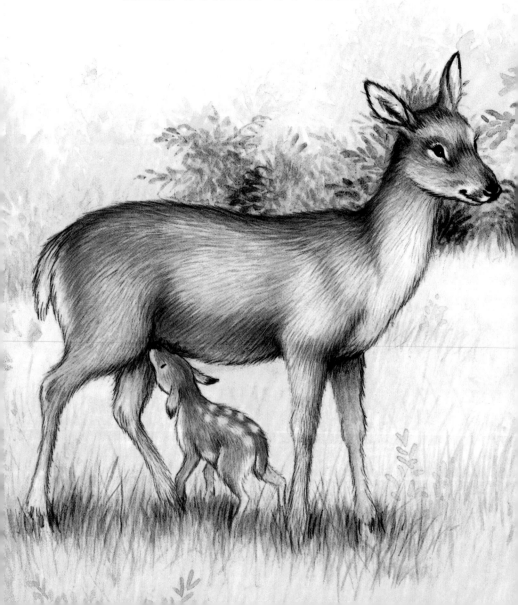

Mama watches
baby so
her little one
won't slip and fall.

Mama loves
her little cubs
and watches
as you roll and play.

You are learning
all the tricks
that you will need
to hunt one day.

Mama loves you,
little one,
and stays with you
both night and day.

When her little one
gets hot,
Mama shoots
a cooling spray.

Mama loves.

Mama loves you,
little one.
You hang onto
her furry back.

Then she climbs
a leafy tree
to get you both
a little snack.

Mama keeps
her joey safe
inside her pouch
all warm and snug.

Mama flies
into the night

and returns to give
her pup a hug.

Mama loves.

Mama loves you,
little kit,
and lifts you gently
by the scruff.

Mama loves her
pack of cubs
and scolds you
when you play too rough.

Mama loves you,
little pup,
born snowy white
so you can hide.

Mama takes
her little babies
for a warm
and cozy ride.

Mama loves.

Holding, sharing,
scolding, caring,
Mama watches
while you grow.

Duckling, doe,
pup, kit, or kitten,
Mama loves
her baby so!

Mama cares
for you until
you are big
and smart and grown.

And maybe one day
you will have . . .

. . . a little baby
of your own!

Mama loves.

BRIGHT and EARLY BOOKS for BEGINNING Beginners®